TIME HUNTERS

GLADIATOR CLASH

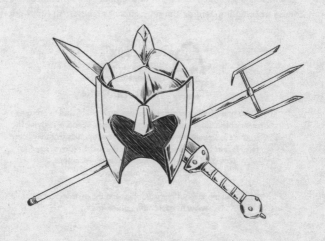

First published in Great Britain by HarperCollins *Children's Books* in 2013
HarperCollins *Children's Books* is a division of HarperCollins*Publishers* Ltd,
77-85 Fulham Palace Road, Hammersmith, London, W6 8JB.

The HarperCollins website address is: www.harpercollins.co.uk

1

Text © Hothouse Fiction Limited 2013
Illustrations © HarperCollins *Children's Books*, 2013
Illustrations by Dynamo

ISBN 978-0-00-794084-4

Printed and bound in England by Clays Ltd, St Ives plc

MIX
Paper from
responsible sources
FSC **FSC C007454**
www.fsc.org

CHRIS BLAKE

TiME HUNTERS

GLADIATOR CLASH

HarperCollins *Children's Books*

CONTENTS

With special thanks to
Marnie Stanton-Riches

PROLOGUE

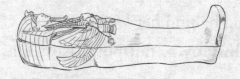

Five thousand years ago

Princess Isis and her pet cat, Cleo, stood outside the towering carved gates to the Afterlife. It had been rotten luck to fall off a pyramid and die at only ten years of age, but Isis wasn't worried – the Afterlife was meant to be great. People were dying to go there, after all! Her mummy's wrappings were so uncomfortable she couldn't wait a second longer to get in, get her body back and wear normal clothes again.

"Oi, Aaanuuubis, Anubidooby!" Isis shouted impatiently. "When you're ready, you old dog!"

Cleo started to claw Isis's shoulder. Then she yowled, jumping from Isis's arms and cowering behind her legs.

"Calm down, fluffpot," Isis said, bending to stroke her pet. "He can't exactly woof me to death!" The princess laughed, but froze when she stood up. Now she understood what Cleo had been trying to tell her.

Looming up in front of her was the enormous jackal-headed god of the Underworld himself, Anubis. He was so tall that Isis's neck hurt to look up at him. He glared down his long snout at her with angry red eyes. There was nothing pet-like about him. Isis gulped.

"'WHEN YOU'RE READY, YOU OLD DOG?'" Anubis growled. "'ANUBIDOOBY?'"

Isis gave the god of the Underworld a winning smile and held out five shining amulets. She had been buried with them so she could give them to Anubis to gain entry to the Afterlife. There was a sixth amulet too – a gorgeous green one. But Isis had hidden it under her arm. Green *was* her favourite colour, and surely Anubis didn't need all six.

Except the god didn't seem to agree. His fur bristled in rage. "FIVE? Where is the sixth?" he demanded.

Isis shook her head. "I was only given five," she said innocently.

To her horror, Anubis grabbed the green amulet from its hiding place. "You little LIAR!" he bellowed.

Thunder started to rumble. The ground shook. Anubis snatched all six amulets and tossed them into the air. With a loud crack and a flash of lightning, they vanished.

"You hid them from me!" he boomed. "Now I have hidden them from you – in the most dangerous places throughout time."

Isis's bandaged shoulders drooped in despair. "So I c-c-can't come into the Afterlife then?"

"Not until you have found each and every

10

one. But first, you will have to get out of this…" Anubis clicked his fingers. A life-sized pottery statue of the goddess Isis, whom Isis was named after, appeared before him.

Isis felt herself being sucked into the statue, along with Cleo. "What are you doing to me?" she yelled.

"You can only escape if somebody breaks the statue," Anubis said. "So you'll have plenty of time to think about whether trying to trick the trickster god himself was a good idea!"

The walls of the statue closed around Isis, trapping her and Cleo inside. The sound of Anubis's evil laughter would be the last sound they would hear for a long, long time…

CHAPTER 1
THE MUMMY

Squeak-thump, squeak-thump, squeak-thump.
Tom Sullivan loved the noise that his trainers made on the shiny floor of the museum. He drank in the smell of wood polish and three-thousand-year-old dust. All the lights were off, apart from those in the display cabinets. All the visitors had gone home. It was just him and Dad.

He reached his dad's office. It was on the first floor, at the end of the Ancient Greece section. The brass nameplate on the door said 'Dr James Sullivan, Archaeologist'.

"One day I'll have one just like it," Tom said to himself. "'Tom Sullivan, History Genius'. Ha!"

He knocked on the door.

"Hi, Dad, will you be long?" Tom asked.

Dad was poring over a sheaf of papers, which were scattered across his untidy desk. "Eh?" he replied.

"Do I have time to explore a bit more?" Tom said.

Dad looked up at him, his bright blue eyes staring out blankly from behind his glasses. "Oh, I'm not hungry, thanks," he said. "I don't like cheese and pickle." He turned his attention back to the papers.

Tom knew his dad was lost in a world of his own, full of pyramids and Romans and Vikings. "I'm off to fight with some gladiators now, Dad," he said. "Maybe some cavemen too."

"That's nice," Dad mumbled.

Tom wandered through the familiar corridors, peering into the display cases of his favourite exhibits. In the hall of Ancient Greece, he admired the feathered Greek army helmets. In the Viking section, he marvelled at the shields and swords covered in strange letters. As he walked through the hall of Medieval Britain, he waved at some models of men wearing chainmail. Finally,

saving the best until last, he went down the stairs to the Ancient Egyptian section.

Tom loved history and liked to pretend he could travel through time. He lunged towards a brightly painted sarcophagus, using his pen as a sword. "Watch out, pharaoh!" he told the exhibit behind the glass. "I'm a deadly swordsman from the future. Your armies will never defeat me!"

Then, with flailing arms, he started to fight off a band of imaginary Ancient Egyptian attackers, running backwards as if he was being chased.

Tom stumbled and tripped, only noticing the statue labelled 'Goddess Isis' when it was too late. He smacked into it at full force.

The statue wobbled to the right, then it rocked back to the left. Tom rushed forward to save it. "Nooo…!" he cried. But he was too late. The statue toppled on to the floor and smashed into a million pieces.

"Uh oh," Tom gulped. "Dad's going to kill me! The museum's going to kill me! Everyone's going to kill me!"

Tom's heart pounded in his chest as he stared at the mess. There were pottery fragments everywhere. Then something very strange began to happen. The bits started to move and shake.

Tom gasped as five fingers reached out from what was left of the statue. The fingers were wrapped in dirty, torn bandages. Like an Egyptian mummy! Tom stared in shock as the fingers stretched out into a hand, opening and closing as if it was trying to grab him. The hand was followed by a wrist, then an arm...

Suddenly a whole, groaning, child-sized mummy sprang from the wreckage. The shape of some sort of mummified animal stood next to it. Both were wrapped head to toe in crusty shreds of cloth, the loose ends flapping as they moved. They looked at Tom and started walking towards him.

"Aaaargh! Don't hurt me!" Tom cried.

But to his surprise the bandaged animal started to purr and then circle round his leg in a friendly manner.

Tom stared down at it. "Oh my gosh! Is that *really* a cat?" he asked in disbelief.

"Yes, of course! It's *my* cat, Cleo!" the mummy said, with a young girl's voice.

The mummy stood up tall, which, Tom noticed, wasn't as tall as him, and straightened its back with a crack. A cloud of dust billowed round the mummy and wafted to the floor, as if someone had beaten a grimy rug with a stick.

"Y-you spoke!" Tom said, wiping his sweaty palms on his school trousers.

The mummy folded its arms. "Well, of course I spoke! What did you expect me to do?"

"Er... but... I can understand you."

"I'm not surprised. Father always said I was special," the mummy sniffed. "That's why he named me after the goddess of magic. My name's Princess Isis Amun-Ra. I'm ten. Who are you?"

Tom scratched his head in exactly the same way his dad had done. "I'm Tom," he said.

The ragged Egyptian princess frowned. "Just Tom? You don't have a title?"

"Sorry if that's not good enough for you," said Tom, slightly annoyed.

"I suppose it'll have to be," Isis said. She picked up the scrawny cat mummy. "We've been stuck inside that statue for a zillion, billion years. Cleo's not much of a talker, unfortunately. I don't think I've ever been so bored."

Tom looked properly at Isis. She didn't seem quite so scary now that he knew she was just a ten year old like him. *Even though she looks in worse shape than my great-grandma and smells weird*, he thought. But, despite the fact that he was fascinated by this mummy-girl, Tom started to edge towards the door. He had seen films about mummys coming to life and he knew they liked to eat brains.

"Look," he said. "I'm going to have to go home very soon. So... it was nice meeting you. Bye!"

"You can't just leave me here. Take me with you," Isis commanded, putting a hand on her hip.

"No way!" Tom said. "You're an Ancient Egyptian mummy. My mum will go nuts if you drop bits of bandage all over my bedroom."

"Bandage? My father was King of Egypt. These are *regal wrappings*, I'll have you know!" Isis snapped.

"Look, Your Royal Dustiness, I'm a lowly human boy with a brand-new carpet and a mum who doesn't care much for mess. So that kind of rules out grotty, ancient house guests – even princesses."

Clomp, clomp, clomp. Suddenly, Tom heard footsteps getting closer.

"Dad's coming!" he said. "Quick! Hide!"

Isis shook her head. "Hide? You must be joking! I've only just got out of that statue. I'm not hiding away again."

"Tom!" Dad called out.

In a panic, Tom glanced around the room. For a second he thought about bundling Isis and Cleo into the shadows. But that would never work. Isis was rooted to the spot, arms

21

folded. Cleo wrapped herself around Isis's ankles. Tom made do with hastily kicking some of the broken pieces of pottery behind a nearby display case.

As Dad walked in, Tom stood in front of Isis and Cleo, desperately trying to make himself big enough to hide them both.

"Ah, there you are!" Dad said. "Having fun?"

Tom looked at his dad's face. He didn't seem to have seen Isis or Cleo, even though they were both standing right behind Tom.

"Yep," he said.

Then Isis stepped forward and waved at his dad. Tom's heart flipped over in his chest. He tried hopping to one side to hide her again.

"I'll be ready to go in five," Dad said. "OK?" Then he shuffled off back to his office as though nothing unusual was going on.

Tom breathed out slowly. "I don't believe it. Dad didn't even notice you. It was like you were... invisible!"

"Well, that decides it," Isis said merrily. "We're coming home with you, whether you like it or not." She clapped her hands together in a cloud of dust. "Lead the way! I haven't got all day, you know."

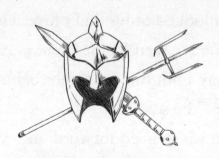

CHAPTER 2
ROMAN HOLIDAY

"Eek!" Isis shrieked, shrinking back in fear.
"You didn't tell me you were a sorceror."

"I'm not," Tom said with a sigh, as he
switched his bedroom light on and off.
"It's just a light."

Isis slowly stepped into Tom's bedroom,
looking round it curiously. The ride home
from the museum had been interesting, as
Isis was convinced that the car was a magic,
horseless chariot. Tom had tried to fill Isis in

on everything that had h[...] died, but the Egyptian prin[...] questions about the modern [...] was exhausted from his atter[...] everything from electricity to [...]

he said. "[...]
thous[...]

"I tell you what, let's Google a few things on the computer," Tom suggested. "Maybe we can find out more about your world too."

Tom sat at his desk and hit a button on the keyboard. The bright colours of the monitor lit the room.

Isis jumped up and cowered behind Tom. "It's a demon from the Underworld come to get me!" she shouted.

Tom laughed. "It's OK," he said. "It's just my computer."

Tapping away on his keyboard, fact by fact, Tom unravelled Isis's past.

"So you're from Ancient Egypt in 2800 BC,"

hat makes you almost five
...nd years old." Tom whistled softly.

"Let me see!" Isis said, looking over his
shoulder. "Does it say that I was a brilliant
dancer and could play the harp better than
anyone else in the Nile delta?"

Suddenly, the ground beneath them
rumbled and the air started to whip around
the room like a mysterious whirlwind.

"Is this another modern invention?" Isis
asked nervously.

"N-n-no," Tom stammered. "Not that I
know of!"

"SILENCE, children!" a voice boomed.

Tom peered into the gloom and saw two
red eyes glowing menacingly at him. He
shrank back in horror.

Isis swung around to face the owner of the
voice as he stepped out of the shadows.

"Hello, Anubis," she said. "You didn't think I'd ever get out of that statue, did you? Well, never underestimate a princess."

Tom looked up… at the god of the Underworld! He recognised the jackal-headed god from pictures he had seen in his dad's books.

"Little Isis Amun-Ra," Anubis said in a haughty voice. "Still cheeky after five thousand years? Well, prepare yourself. Your challenge is about to begin."

Anubis folded his arms across his bare chest, raising an eyebrow at Tom. "You freed the princess from her statue, boy. Now you are destined by the gods to accompany Isis Amun-Ra on her journey through time to find her amulets."

Frustration burst out of Tom in a flurry of angry words. "Now just hold on! That's not fair!" He thumped the desk and glared at Anubis and Isis. "I've got caught up in this by accident—"

"You don't have a choice," Anubis growled. "To find the amulets, you will both journey far back in time to some of the most dangerous moments in history. Time will stand still while you are away, boy. Your parents will know nothing of your adventures."

Tom's ears pricked up at the word 'history'. He loved reading about history. Here was a chance to go on a treasure hunt through history and see it with his own eyes, even if he *did* have to go with a bossy Ancient Egyptian princess. It was the chance of a lifetime!

Anubis held his long arms wide and the strange wind started to whip up again.

"Prepare for your first journey," he said.

Tom, Isis and Cleo, nervous of where
they might end up, held hands and paws in
a circle. The powerful tornado
started to curl around them,
pulling them out of Tom's
world and into the
unknown.

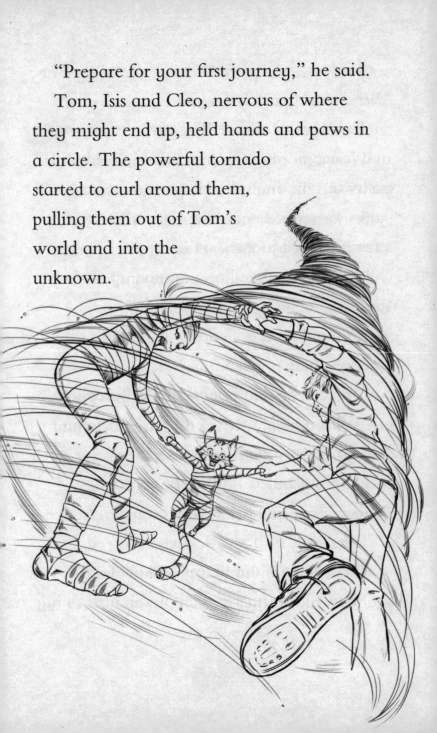

★

"Where are we?" Isis asked.

Tom looked round. They were standing in a long, gloomy, stone corridor, lined with archways on one side. He peered into a sunlit, dusty courtyard beyond. Men were stretching and jogging on the spot.

"It looks like they're warming up to do sports or something," he said.

A young man appeared, walking briskly towards them.

"Hello," he said brightly. "I'm Josephus."

"What's your title?" Isis said, eyeing his grubby, short toga suspiciously.

Josephus smiled. "Why, I'm a slave, of course!" he chuckled. "Are you new?"

Tom and Isis nodded. Cleo meowed.

"Er... what is this place?" asked Tom.

"This is the city's biggest gladiator training

school, owned by my master, Atillius!" the young man explained.

Tom frowned, deep in thought. He looked at the strange clothes he and Isis were both wearing – simple tunics and sandals. And hadn't he spied a man through the arches dressed in the long folds of a toga? Yes! Gladiators... slaves... togas...

"We're in Ancient Rome!" he shouted. "Brilliant!"

Tom suddenly wondered how it was possible that he and Josephus could understand each other. He didn't speak any Latin aside from a few words his dad had taught him.

"It must be part of Anubis's magic," Tom said aloud.

But Isis seemed to be a million miles away, staring at her hand in amazement. She started patting her arms and legs in delight. Tom suddenly realised why — instead of being wrapped up as a mouldy mummy, she was made of flesh and blood again.

Isis grinned at Tom. "I'm alive!" she cried, feeling the long, black plaits of her hair. "No more horrible bandages!" Then she looked down at Cleo, who had transformed back into a sleek cat, covered in tabby stripes.

"Cleo! My little fluffpot!" Isis said, scooping Cleo up into a hug.

"Er, I hate to interrupt," Josephus said, "but you're meant to be training to fight as gladiators right now."

Isis stuck her nose in the air. "Fight? But I'm a princess."

Josephus pointed at the men in the courtyard. "Not any more you're not. Everyone here is a prisoner or a slave. Where have you come from anyway?"

"Egypt," Tom said, pointing at Isis. "And Britain," he added, gesturing to himself.

Josephus shrugged. "The Roman Army doesn't usually send child prisoners to fight," he said. "But then, they're so cruel, nothing they do surprises me these days."

Tom gulped. "Cruel?"

Isis was offended. "Prisoner? *I'm* a

prisoner? I insist you free me right now!"

"*You* shouldn't even be here," Josephus said, prodding Isis in the shoulder. "No girls. No cats. Don't worry, the soldiers will throw you out as soon as they see you."

Isis tossed her plaits and balled her fists. "We're on a very important mission. We *must* stay here together."

"Please help us," Tom begged Josephus. "We really can't be separated."

"I suppose I don't owe the Romans anything," Josephus said with a shrug. "OK, I'll help. First, we must disguise Princess Bossyboots here as a boy."

"A boy!?" Isis shrieked in disgust.

"Shhhh!" Tom and Josephus both hissed.

Josephus pushed the three travellers into a shadowy alcove and started to wipe off the kohl from Isis's eyes with a rag.

"Get off me! You smell of rotten vegetables," Isis cried, batting him away.

"Just keep still, Princess Bossyboots," Tom said. He grinned as he tied back her long hair out of sight.

Josephus ducked into a nearby cupboard and emerged with rattling chains. "Sorry. I have to put chains on you, like the others, otherwise the guards will think you're trying to escape." He shackled them both at the wrists and ankles and pushed them, clanking, down the colonnade.

"What about my cat, Cleo?" Isis asked.

"Animals aren't allowed in the training ground. She'll get killed if she stays here," said Josephus. "She can stay in my quarters, where the other animals are kept. Don't worry, I'll look after her."

He steered Tom and Isis into a noisy

room with a barred door. Tom saw that it
was packed with chained prisoners, both
young and old, chattering away in a variety
of languages he'd never heard before.
Some had pale skin, some had dark skin.
Everyone wore different clothes. Clearly they
came from all over the world. They were
shovelling food into their
mouths with their
shackled hands.

"You're lucky – you're in time for breakfast. Try to blend in," Josephus said, looking doubtfully at Isis, as he carried Cleo off in his arms.

Isis and Tom sat on the stone floor in silence, taking in their surroundings with wide eyes. Tom helped himself to a piece of bread.

"I hope Cleo's all right," Isis whispered to Tom. "At least she can cuddle up to the other animals."

Just then a roar echoed around the barracks that made Tom shudder.

"Oh no! What was that? It didn't sound very cuddly," Isis whimpered.

One of the other prisoners leaned over. "That's the wild animals," he said glumly. "Sounded like a lion. Sometimes it's tigers, bears... anything that can tear your toenails off with its teeth." He stroked his stubbly chin thoughtfully. "I still can't decide which is worse."

"What do you mean?" Tom asked, gulping.

The prisoner shrugged. "Being killed by a gladiator's sword or eaten by lions. What's the better way to die?"

"I don't even want to think about it, thanks!" said Tom.

The prisoner looked grim-faced. "Well, you should. Because none of us will make it out of here alive."

CHAPTER 3
GLADIATOR TRAINING

"We need a plan. We've got to find the amulet and leave this place before we have to fight anyone," Tom said.

Isis held up her hands and rattled her chains. "We can't exactly go for a stroll, can we, Professor Smartypants?" she said.

Tom scratched his head and tried to remember everything he knew about gladiators. "Look," he said, "gladiators fight with swords and shields, or daggers and spears. They'll make us practise so they can't keep us locked up forever. At least the food is OK."

Isis peered down at the other prisoners' plates and snorted. "Pah! Oats and beans? These Romans haven't got a clue. Our Egyptian fighters were tough and lean. They fought with their hands and feet, not wobbling around with a sword and a belly full of porridge!"

Tom shrugged. "So, any thoughts on where the amulet might be, oh warrior princess?"

"I've no idea," Isis said. "But I do have something that might help us. Look!" She waved her hand in front of Tom's face.

"I know, I know," said Tom. "You're not a mummy any more. But how does that help us?"

"No, silly. My ring," said Isis, pointing
to the gold ring on her finger. It was in the
shape of a scarab beetle, and on it
was a hierogylph
of a woman on
a throne.

"That's who
I'm named after
– the goddess
Isis," explained
Isis. "She's the
goddess of magic and children, and protector
of the dead. I wore this ring all throughout
my life. I was even buried in it."

Tom studied the ring closely. "Cool! I've
never seen a ring like that before," he said.

"Finally!" Isis harrumphed. "Something
Professor Know-It-All *doesn't* know about."

"Well, go on then," said Tom. "We're

both kids, and you're dead. Let's face it – we could certainly do with some help!"

Frowning in concentration, Isis said, "Oh, magical scarab. Oh, lovely goddess Isis. Will you please, please, pretty-please help me find my amulet?"

Suddenly a whirring noise, like flapping insect wings, came from the scarab. Silvery letters started to float out of the ring and into the air:

If you're in a sticky spot,
Don't be glum! Panic not!
Cheerful is the one you need to find.
Triumphant after thirteen fights,
The middle of his shield so bright,
Seek the treasure there, don't be blind.

"It's a riddle!" Tom said, after reading the

words. His eyes narrowed as he pondered the clues. "This has got to be about one of the gladiators, if it mentions fighting and a shield. But which one?"

Isis looked at her ring. "Do you think we're searching for someone who's sticky?" she asked, wrinkling her nose. "Yuck! Maybe it's someone who doesn't wash their hands after eating. A gladiator called Stickius Smellius."

Just then, a tall, burly, bald man carrying a whip opened the door to the prison cell with a crash. The other prisoners held their chains up for him to unlock. When it was Tom and Isis's turn, the man raised his eyebrow.

"Children?" he said. "We've never had children before." His stern face cracked into a greedy grin. "Why, the crowd are going to go crazy for children fighting in the arena! Imagine that!"

The man ushered Tom, Isis and the rest of the prisoners into the training-ground courtyard. The sun blazed down on the stone buildings. The burning heat bounced up off the sandy ground.

When they were all assembled, he shouted, "My name is Rufus. I'm here to train you as gladiators. I'll put you into five groups where you will learn different ways of fighting. You will need to become fearsome warriors and the fittest of athletes."

Isis clapped her hands together and turned to Tom. "I'm just brilliant at athletics! And archery! And you should see me on a horse."

Tom groaned. "Is there anything you *can't* do?"

Rufus started to hand out weapons, shields and armour to the small groups of prisoners. Tom was put in the *scissores* group.

44

He thought about what he could do with scissors. They were fine for cutting paper, but as a weapon they'd be pretty useless. Surely gladiators didn't fight with scissors?

But the weapon Rufus thrusted into Tom's hand was made up of two short, sharp swords fixed together at the hilt. They didn't look anything like ordinary scissors.

Rufus showed Tom how he was meant to capture his enemy between the blades.

He practised using the scissors on a straw dummy shaped like a man.

"Cut, cut, cut!" Tom shouted gleefully to the other prisoners.

They looked at him with sour faces.

"Oh, come on, guys!" Tom said. "This is fun!"

After only ten minutes though, he found his arms had started to tremble under the weight of the clumsy blades. The blistering heat was tiring him.

Wondering how Isis was getting on, he looked over to her group. As one of the *sagittariuses*, she was shooting arrows with a bow from the saddle of a chestnut-coloured horse. Tom wondered if she was struggling like him.

"Yoohoo, Tom!" Isis shouted over to him. "Look at me!" She pinged off her practice arrows one after another, and hit the target every time. Each time she shot an arrow, she flashed Tom a triumphant look.

During a rest break, Tom and Isis sat together briefly.

"Any more ideas about the riddle, then?" Isis asked, gobbling down some dried apricots.

Tom swigged from a jug full of horrible warm water. "Yes," he said. "*Triumphant in thirteen fights* means we're looking for a really experienced gladiator. If he's won that many battles he must be a kind of hero."

Before they could discuss the riddle further, Rufus put the trainees into new groups. Tom and Isis were in the *retiarius* group, where they fought with nets and tridents. Whenever they could fight each other, they did. It was their only chance to talk – and make sure they didn't get hurt.

"It's obvious the amulet is the *treasure* in his shield," Tom said, whizzing a net around his head.

"But who is this hero?" Isis asked, dodging out of the way.

"And what's there to be cheerful about?" Tom asked.

At lunchtime, most of the prisoners rested.
Tom would have liked to take a nap, but Isis
was worried about Cleo.

"My little fluffpot will be missing me,"
she said. "I need to give her a cuddle."
So Isis and Tom slipped away to find
Josephus.

The musty smell of animals led them down to the gloomy basement beneath the barracks. There they found Josephus filling troughs with water.

"So this is where the roaring was coming from!" Tom said.

From inside the cages came growling and snapping.

Josephus chuckled. "Come and meet Cleo's new neighbours," he said.

Tom gulped as he saw enormous, shaggy-maned lions prowling around one cage. Their teeth were like daggers. Directly opposite, a tail swished in the gloom. Tom peered to get a closer look, then yelped as he made out the wide, muscular body of an alligator crawling out of a small pond within the cage. It snapped its jaws full of razor-sharp teeth.

"The Roman Army brings back all sorts of exotic animals from their foreign campaigns," Josephus explained. "They use them to fight against each other and against the gladiators."

"Cleo! Cleopatra!" Isis shouted. "What have these horrible animals done to you?"

Mewing and the padding of small paws echoed off the walls as Cleo scampered over to Isis.

"My fluffy love!" Isis scooped up her cat into her arms. "I thought you'd been eaten!" She stroked Cleo's stripy fur. Cleo purred happily.

"Mind out!" Josephus shouted, pushing past Tom. He was carrying a large bucket full of smelly, slippery meat. As he pulled out what looked like the leg of a cow, the lions started to fling their heavy bodies against the bars, snarling and clawing at the meat. The alligator snapped its jaws and thrashed its tail against the pen.

"They're hungry, all right!" Josephus said.

Cleo jumped down from Isis's arms.

"Cleo, no!" Isis shouted.

Tom almost couldn't bear to look as Cleo walked over to the cages and started to hiss at the dangerous beasts. She swiped at the lions and alligator with her own sharp little claws. But instead of tearing the cat to pieces, the wild animals backed into the shadowy corners of their cages, whimpering and shaking.

"Why! That's the strangest thing I've ever seen," Josephus said, scratching his head. "How can a little cat like that scare wild beasts? Those creatures would normally snap her up!"

"They're frightened of you, Cleo! They must know you're royal!" Isis beamed. "That's my girl! Top cat!"

"I don't think they know she's royal," Tom whispered to Isis. "They must know she's undead."

Cleo haughtily stuck her tail in the air and started hungrily scoffing a chunk of meat.

Isis breathed a sigh of relief. "Oh well, I certainly don't need to worry about you down here," she said, stroking Cleo under her chin.

Josephus turned to Isis with a raised eyebrow. There was something about his expression that made Isis gulp.

"Cleo's all right," he said. "But how will the two of you fare when it's time to fight in the arena?"

CHAPTER 4
ANUBIS DROPS IN

"Ow! My legs are killing me!" Tom said, as they shuffled back into the prisoner quarters.

Isis stretched her back and groaned. "I don't think I was this stiff after five thousand years of being trapped in a statue." She straightened out, holding her nose. "And it stinks like a camel's bed in here."

"Are you sure it's not you?" Tom asked. "You *are* quite old."

"Ha ha, very funny!"

The door clanged open, flooding the prisoners' room with a sudden blinding shaft of light that made Tom squint.

Rufus burst in. "Greetings, gladiators!" he cried. "I have exciting news for you."

Nobody seemed excited. At all. Tom looked around at the tired, dirty faces of the other prisoners. Everyone was covered in cuts and bright purple bruises.

Rufus pointed his coiled-up whip at the prisoners. "Atillius has just announced that there will be a grand show in two days' time. Which means you will get your first fight."

The prisoners all started to grumble.

Rufus cracked the whip. "Hey! Stop whinging, you ungrateful donkeys! Atillius is spending a fortune to make this show bigger and better than ever." He folded his meaty arms and glared at the prisoners. "Guess who has agreed to fight? None other than Hilarus! You lot will be the warm-up acts before his fight!"

Each and every prisoner started to groan in despair. Some even broke into great sobs.

Isis elbowed the man next to her in the ribs. "Who's Hilary?" she asked him.

The man moved away from her, rubbing his side. "How can you not have heard of Hilarus?" he asked. "He's the most famous gladiator in the Roman Empire. He's won thirteen fights in a row. Huge crowds will be coming to see him."

"So why's everyone moaning?" Isis sniffed.

The man chuckled bitterly and shook his head at her. "In the arena, they fight to the death."

Tom and Isis exchanged nervous glances. Gladiator training was tough, but at least nobody had been trying to kill them!

"We've got to find the amulet soon," Isis whispered to Tom in alarm. "Or else we'll end up in the arena."

Rufus cracked his whip until the grim chatter stopped.

"You should be thankful! This is the most excitement you mangy lot will ever see!" he shouted. "There's going to be parades, musicians, spectacles... animals too."

The door clanged as Josephus walked in. Everybody turned around as he strode to the front.

"Er, perhaps not the animals," he said to Rufus, wringing his hands.

Rufus's tanned face wrinkled into an almighty frown. "But Atillius definitely wants to include them in a fight."

Josephus shook his head. "Sorry. There's something wrong with them. They're acting all timid like mice; it's as though they've seen a ghost. I've tried stoking them up. I even threatened to turn the alligator into a pair of sandals. But they've lost their bite!" He shrugged. "They would make a truly poor show, I'm afraid."

"Well, Atillius will just have to leave them out," Rufus said.

Meanwhile, the prisoners had started to panic.

"I'm going to grab the heavy, shiny armour!" one yelled. "A sword won't get through that."

"Are you mad?" cried another. "Swords cut through everything. The only hope of escape is dodging the blows with fancy footwork."

Tom, who had been listening carefully to all Rufus said, couldn't wait to pull Isis to one side. He felt like his heart would burst if he didn't get the words out.

"Hey, remember the riddle said *cheerful is the one you need to find*?" he whispered. "Well, I've worked it out. Guess what the Latin for cheerful is!"

Isis shook her head.

"Hilarus!"

"The other prisoners say he's undefeated in thirteen fights," Isis said.

"Exactly!" Tom beamed at Isis and gave her the thumbs up. "He's our man."

"So if the amulet is in his shield, we've got to get close to him in the arena," Isis said. "Which means—"

"We'll have to fight the most fearsome gladiator in the whole of the Roman Empire," Tom finished. He swallowed hard and felt his spine tingle with dread. If they could get their hands on the amulet, they'd be whisked back to the safety of Tom's bedroom. But how on earth were they going to get close enough to Hilarus's shield without getting hurt?

Suddenly, the ground started to rumble beneath them.

Isis gasped. "What's happening?"

"I think it's an earthquake," Tom said, feeling tremors under his feet. "Quick – take cover!"

As the two of them scrambled into a

corner, the stone floor cracked, then opened up. Anubis's jackal head burst out of the ground. It was almost the full height of the room. His fierce eyes glared at them in an alarming shade of red.

The other prisoners continued to talk about the gladiatorial show, unaware of the terrifying Egyptian god in the room.

Anubis sneered at Tom and Isis as they huddled together.

"You're not having *fun*, are you?" He blasted them with his foul doggy breath.

"N-no!" Isis said, covering her nose with her tunic.

Anubis started to heave with unkind laughter. "You'll be torn from limb to limb in the arena!"

Isis stood tall, fists balled and with her chin stuck out in grim determination. "My opponents had better train hard before they square up to *this* princess."

"Ha! The young princess is deluded as usual! Two children against the best fighter in history? You don't stand a chance."

Tom's teeth were chattering with fear as he thought about having to fight in the arena. "Can I just ask?" he said in a small voice, looking up at Anubis. "Why are you being so horrible to us? Why can't you find your own amulets? You're a god, after all."

Anubis fixed Tom with his glowing red eyes. "She hasn't told you, has she?"

Isis shook her head and blushed bright red.

"Told me what?" Tom asked.

He looked over at Isis but her large brown eyes were fixed firmly on her sandal-clad feet.

"Princess Isis tried to steal an amulet from me," Anubis barked. "If I had my way, I wouldn't let her into the Afterlife at all. But even gods have rules. If she has the payment, I must let her through."

"So why don't you?" Tom asked. "You know where the amulets are. Just let her through now. Surely trapping her in the statue was punishment enough?"

Anubis scowled, showing his razor-sharp fangs. "What would be the fun in that, boy? Who knows? If she survives the challenges, she may even learn her lesson. If you *both* survive, that is!" He started to laugh nastily.

The ground trembled again. Tom marvelled that the other prisoners didn't even look round to see where the noise was coming from.

"Remember, Isis!" Anubis growled. "No amulets, no Afterlife!"

"I know! I know!" Isis said through gritted teeth.

"Now, I do hope you both enjoy Ancient Rome," Anubis boomed. "Because if you don't find the first amulet, you'll be stuck here forever!"

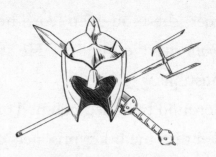

CHAPTER 5
TRY OUTS

"Imagine being torn limb from limb," Tom
said above the snoring of the other prisoners.
He shivered at the thought. "Ouch."

Isis yawned. "Go to sleep, Tom! Rufus
will be in here soon enough."

Tom propped himself up on his elbow.
"Sleep? You're joking, right? I can't get
Anubis's words out of my head." He sat up,
hugging his knees to his body. "Do you really
think they do that sort of thing?" he asked.

"Surely they spare you if you surrender? Not that *I* would surrender, of course."

In the gloomy light of the breaking dawn, Isis stuck out her chin. "Well, nobody's tearing my limbs off. I waited five thousand years to get a body again. I'm not going to let some gladiator ruin it."

Tom straightened himself out, feeling more determined. "If I die in that arena and Mum finds out, she'll kill me!" he said. "You and I will just have to work as a team."

"A team?" Isis squeaked. "Princesses don't really do teams. By rights, you should just throw down your life for me."

Tom tutted and shook his head. "Then how will you get your amulets? You might not like to admit it, but you do need my help. Plus, this *is* all your fault in the first place!"

"Oh, yes, of course, we're in this together," Isis said, quickly changing tack. "A team we shall be! Nobody beats Isis Amun-Ra and her trusty friend, Tom!"

Suddenly, there was a crash as Rufus flung open the barred door.

"Get up, you lazy lot!" he shouted, brandishing his whip. "Training time!"

Everyone in the cell started to stir and stretch.

Isis held her nose. "Ugh! I'd forgotten that prisoners smell so bad."

Tom wrinkled his nose at her. "You don't smell of flowers either, Your Royal Ponginess."

When they had all gathered round, Rufus rubbed his shiny, bald head. He seemed excited.

"More news about the show!" Rufus said, grinning like a shark. "Hilarus will fight *catervarii*, which means he'll fight on his own against a group of gladiators. We'll be selecting five of you lucky lot to take on the famous Hilarus in person!"

All around, Tom heard groans coming from the men.

"It's not fair!" one man cried. "Hilarus is too good."

"How are we supposed to survive that?" another jeered.

"You're not!" Rufus answered cheerfully. "Anyone matched against the great hero can expect to die. That's what the crowds have come to see."

Tom caught Isis's eye and winked.

"This is our big chance," he whispered. "You and me. We'll get picked to fight against Hilarus and get that amulet, or danger's not my middle name."

"*Is* danger your middle name?" Isis asked, toying with her chains.

Tom shook his head. "No, it's Nigel."

Outside, Rufus stood on top of a wooden trunk full of weapons and clapped his hands together.

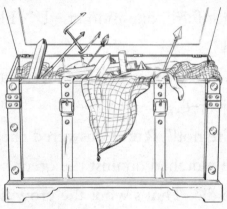

"Listen up! I'm going to hold trials to pick the five best fighters to face Hilarus," he announced. "So pick your best category – you can only try out for one."

Once again, a ripple of complaint moved around the prisoners.

Tom eyed a tall, skinny young man, who was standing close by, whispering to an older man. The older man had the biggest muscles Tom had ever seen.

"It's too dangerous," the young man said to the older man. "I really don't want to get picked. What should I do?"

The older man leaned forward and whispered, "Pretend to be useless. The more rubbish you are with a sword, the less likely it is you'll get picked."

Tom nudged Isis and pulled her to one side. "We've got to do our best and really stand out," he said. "It might not be so difficult if the others are trying to lose."

As the prisoners were led out to the training ground after breakfast, Tom and Isis talked about what to try out for. It was obvious that Isis should try out as a *sagittarius*,

71

or archer. But Tom wasn't great at any of the categories. He couldn't ride a horse, so it was no use trying out to be a mounted fighter. The scissors were just too heavy for him, and he'd kept getting tangled up in the net.

"I guess I'll try out as a *dimachaerus*," Tom said, not feeling very hopeful.

But he needn't have worried. When the trials began, the other prisoners pretended to have forgotten everything they had learned. Tom watched in disbelief as most of the men spent the morning tripping over their own swords or just simply falling over. The first three places went to the fighters who were the least bad in their groups. Tom and Isis were still waiting to compete. As the minutes ticked by Tom felt more and more nervous. What would happen if they didn't

get chosen? How else would they get close to
Hilarus?

At last it was time for the mounted archers
to try out. Isis, who was already a dab hand
with a bow and an excellent horseman, easily
reached the final three of her group.

Rufus strutted back and forth in front of
Isis and the two grim-faced men who were
left. "I'm going to set a tricky test to decide
between you three," he said. "How about a
little target practice?"

He tied an apple to the top of a pole and
then turned to Isis and the two remaining
men.

"The best shot on horseback from the
opposite end of the courtyard wins their place
in the fight against Hilarus," he said.

The first man galloped up to the firing
point. He aimed his arrow, stretched the

string of his bow back and *ping*! The arrow sailed up through the air, down towards the apple... and missed by a whisker!

Tom let out the breathe he didn't realise he'd been holding in. Isis looked over at him and raised an eyebrow.

The next man to try out wore a bandage around his head.

"Your turn!" Rufus said.

The man looked at him blankly.

"I said, *your turn*!" Rufus growled.

Grasping at his bandaged ear, the man frowned at Rufus and then smiled. "Oh, sorry," he shouted. "I can't hear properly. I got hit on the head by a shield yesterday."

"Good luck," bellowed Isis.

"Eh?" said the man, swivelling around and clonking Isis in the face with his bow.

74

"Ouch!" squealed Isis, rubbing her cheek dramatically.

"Oh, stop being such a baby," said Tom.

"Oops! Sorry, sonny," said the man. As he clumsily climbed up into his saddle, a shower of arrows fell out of his quiver. One sharp point grazed the tip of Tom's toe.

"Ow!" shouted Tom, hopping on one leg.

"*Now* who's acting like a baby," said Isis.

The man rode his horse to the far end of the arena. He bounced around in the saddle, looking like he was going to fall off. When he got to the end of the courtyard, he took his shot. The arrow whizzed through the air and landed with a clatter on the dusty ground several feet to the left of the apple.

Now it was Isis's turn.

"Wish me luck," Isis said as she patted her horse's neck.

75

"You'll be brilliant," Tom said, giving her the most encouraging smile he could muster. He knew that if Isis missed, they would never get the amulet back.

"Well, giddy-up, horsey," Isis said, digging her heels into the side of her mount and breaking into a gallop.

The horse's hooves thundered across the arena, kicking up dust. Tom bit his lip

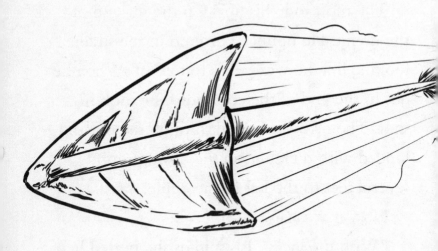

nervously as Isis grabbed an arrow from her quiver and nocked it. She stretched the arrow back against the arch of the bow and released it with a *twang*! As the arrow flew through the air, time seemed to slow down. Was the arrow going a bit too far to the left?

Tom couldn't bear to watch.

CHAPTER 6
ITCHING TO FIGHT

Thwunk! Isis's arrow hit the apple, splitting it in two.

"It seems we've found our archer," Rufus said. "This child will fight against Hilarus!"

Tom cheered and thumped the air. He gave Isis the thumbs up. The other trainees clapped and whistled. Some laughed and wiped their brows dramatically, as though Isis's amazing performance had got them off the hook... for now.

"Your turn," said Isis as she cantered back to Tom. "Good luck."

Tom needed luck, but he thought he might have a secret move that he hoped would be enough to get him chosen as a *catervarii*. A *dimachaerus* fought with two swords, and Tom thought he might just have a chance.

Tom picked up two heavy swords, his heart beating wildly as he thought about what he had to do. His muscles immediately screamed with the weight, his arms were already tired. Tom started to spin around in a circle and the swords lifted up easily. Suddenly, he became just like the blades that whizzed around in Mum's food processor.

"I'm the school champion at doing helicopters," he shouted to Isis.

"*What?*" Isis asked, backing away.

Tom slowed
down and
gradually
came to a stop
without even
stumbling.
"Spinning
round," he
explained.
"I never feel
dizzy. I don't
fall over – even
when I've been on a
roundabout for ages."

"Well, let's just hope you don't fall down now," Isis said. "The winner is the last man standing."

"Don't worry, with my super spinning powers, the momentum will keep the swords in the air. Hilarus won't dare come near me!" Tom smiled at Isis and strode purposefully up to Rufus.

"I want to try out as a *dimachaerus*," Tom said.

Rufus towered above Tom. "You do, do you?" he asked, grinning. "You do know you have to have the heart of a lion, or be as mad as a goat to fight without any armour or a shield? Especially against Hilarus."

Tom gulped. Wearing no armour would make fighting Hilarus even more dangerous. But he didn't have a choice – this was his last chance to get picked.

"I'm serious," Tom said. "Let me try."

Rufus nodded and treated Tom to a nasty smile. "You'll be a small but easy target. The crowd will love it!" He turned to the other trainees. "Any more of you stinking prisoners stupid or brave enough to try out as a *dimachaerus*?" he shouted to the group.

The others hung back in the shade of an archway and edged further into the colonnade. Before Rufus could force them, one other trainee came forward.

"I've heard prisoners who fight bravely are sometimes freed. Is that true?" the man asked.

"Only if the crowd decides they've fought like a hero. It hardly ever happens so I wouldn't bank on it," Rufus said.

The man looked into Rufus's eyes. "Well, if beating Hilarus gives me a chance of being freed, I will try out," he said.

Tom knew this man's name was Marcus. He was young, but a grown-up and much taller and broader than Tom. Marcus stood in his grubby loincloth, with his hands on his hips and his strong legs planted firmly on the ground. Tom could see from the set of his jaw that he was just as determined to win as Tom was.

Tom could feel his heart sinking. This didn't look good.

Isis ran over to his side. "Don't worry, I'm going to help you," she whispered into Tom's ear.

"How can you possibly help me?" Tom asked, sighing.

Isis tutted. "You think you're so clever with your modern science and inventions, Professor Smartypants," she said. "But when I was in Egypt, I learned all about plants and herbs."

"I don't understand," Tom said, running a hand through his dark blond curls. "Are you planning on luring Marcus into a garden to smell the flowers?"

Isis rolled her eyes. "You're such a silly boy! No, there's a plant growing up the fence. See it over there?" She pointed. "It's got leaves that split into three sections. I know exactly what to do with it!"

Tom looked where she was pointing and saw some weeds growing along the edges of the dry, dusty courtyard. He couldn't see how they could possibly help him.

Isis's eyes shone with mischief. Without saying another word, she walked over to the low fence and carefully picked a handful of leaves from the plant she had pointed out.

Tom watched as Isis ambled back across the arena, whistling as though she had just been for a stroll. Pausing near the weapons, she pretended to lace up her sandals. Tom saw her rub the leaves on the handles of two of the swords. She was so quick that nobody seemed to notice her.

"Don't pick those swords," Isis said to Tom, thumping him on the back and looking pleased with herself. Tom could feel her excitement prickle up his arms.

"Right, you two," ordered Rufus. "Let's get this fight over with. Get your equipment and let's begin. The winner will be the last of the *catervarii*."

Tom raced forward and chose the swords that Isis hadn't touched. Marcus picked up his weapons and the bout began. Energy surged through Tom's body. He raised the heavy swords, swiping the air as he looked around for his opponent.

"Watch out, Tom!" Isis cried from the sidelines.

Tom turned to see Marcus hurtling

towards him with both his swords
outstretched. He lunged straight for
Tom's throat with the sword
in his right hand.

Tom leaped backwards, narrowly missing
the lethal blade. He started to spin round
and, sure enough, Marcus started to retreat.

Whacka-whacka-whacka-whacka. Tom spun his swords through the air just like the blades on a helicopter. They made a noise which Tom thought was the coolest thing ever but which Marcus, judging by the shade of green he was turning, found utterly frightening.

"Wheeheeee!" Tom shouted, spinning faster and faster on the spot.

Marcus swiped uselessly in his direction, but even through the blur, Tom could see his opponent was too scared to come closer.

"Go on, Marcus!" one of the trainees shouted. "Slit the boy's gizzard!"

As if buoyed by the support, Marcus came at Tom with a frenzied attack, knocking him over. Their swords clashed at the hilts.

Tom gulped. Although he wasn't dizzy, he was no match for Marcus's superior height and strength. He could feel his sword hand giving way to the force of Marcus's weapon. But then...

"Ow!" Marcus suddenly staggered away. "Ow, my hands! It's unbearable!"

Tom stood and watched as Marcus dropped his swords and started to dance around, rubbing his hands madly against his loincloth.

"By the gods! It itches! Someone make it stop!" Marcus cried, scratching at the palms of his hands.

Tom watched in amazement as Marcus stumbled across the sandy arena to the sidelines. He dunked his hands into a trough of water meant for the horses. The man's palms were bright red.

Tom looked over at Isis, who gave him a wink.

Rufus cracked his whip to get everyone's attention.

"That settles it!" he said. "The boy has won. He will fight Hilarus!"

Tom punched the air and shouted, "YES!" But the smile slid quickly from his face when he suddenly realised what that meant.

Now he'd have to fight against a deadly gladiator, or be stuck in Ancient Rome forever.

CHAPTER 7
IT'S SHOWTIME!

"We need a plan," Tom whispered to Isis. He'd read enough history books to know that you needed a strategy if you wanted to win a battle.

"How about if I distract him with my beauty, then you run in and steal the amulet," Isis suggested.

Tom rolled his eyes. He thought for a moment. "Actually, distracting him isn't a bad idea. How about if I try to make him dizzy with my spinning swords, so you can grab the amulet."

"Sounds good to me," said Isis.

"Come on, you two," Rufus said. "You should have your costumes on by now. It doesn't take all day."

Tom and Isis were standing with the other trainees in a cool antechamber beneath the packed Coliseum. Everyone was strapping on armour, tightening their outfits and arranging the feathers in their helmets. The crowd roared in the seating above.

Isis pointed at Tom's bare chest and loincloth. She started to laugh.

"Next to all these hulking great men in armour, you look like a baby in a nappy!" she teased.

Tom looked at Isis. On her head she wore a pointed helmet. She clutched her bow in her hand. Her quiver full of arrows was slung over her shoulder. She was wearing shiny body armour made from metal scales.

"Well, you look like... a stupid big fish! So there," he said.

Isis opened her mouth to respond but was silenced by Rufus as he thrust a piece of silky material into her free hand. He passed the same thing to Tom.

"What are these?" Tom asked, smoothing the fabric out, and saw that it was a banner of some sort.

"They're sashes. Atillius always likes to advertise his other businesses in front of the arena crowds. He owns you, so you have to do it. Put them on."

Tom frowned as he read the slogan written down the length of the white silky sash. He translated the Latin for Isis.

"'Expandable loincloths. Atillius has got even the biggest bums covered!'" he read. "Hey, Isis! We're going to advertise big pants!"

Tom started to guffaw with laughter as he slipped his sash over his head but Isis stood rooted to the spot, her face crumpled into a thunderous expression.

"I... am... *not*... wearing... *that!*" she spat. She thrust her sash into Tom's hands. "You wear it!"

"I've already got one," Tom said.

"You have a bare chest. You should be thanking me. I'm offering you extra clothes."

Tom looped Isis's sash over the point on her helmet so that it hung down over her face with 'BIGGEST BUM' visible. Several of the other trainees noticed and started cackling with laughter.

Even as Rufus herded the trainees up the stone steps to the arena entrance, Tom and Isis were still squabbling over the sash.

"I command you to wear it!" Isis said, eyes flashing with anger.

As they stumbled into the boiling-hot midday sun of the amphitheatre, Tom and Isis were *still* scuffling.

"I am not wearing your big bum sash," Tom snapped. "I already have my own. And that's that."

Isis tried to lasso Tom with her sash but missed. It fell into the dust between them. People in the crowd were pointing and laughing at them.

Rufus cracked his whip. "Enough! Save your fighting for Hilarus."

The two fell silent.

Tom faced the front and took in his surroundings properly. The huge Coliseum was packed with cheering spectators in rows of seats that seemed to climb all the way up to the blue sky. It reminded Tom of a football stadium.

The fighters were led around the arena by a band. The musicians played a lively tune on instruments that looked a bit like skinny tubas, and long horns that were polished to such a shine that they made Tom squint. There were drums, cymbals and bells, playing a beat that matched the pounding of Tom's heart.

Behind the musicians came the experienced gladiators wearing special show armour made from silver and gold. They would fight before the *catervarii*.

"They look tough," Tom said to Isis. He eyed their rippling muscles enviously.

"Pah! They don't scare me," she said, unimpressed.

Tom stared in awe at their helmets that had jewel-coloured peacock feathers arcing from their foreheads to the nape of their necks. They reminded Tom of the ones in his dad's museum.

Even though he was dressed in a loincloth and Atillius's big bum sash, Tom felt excited to be part of the procession. All of the fighters' weaponry had been polished so

that the sun glinted off the fearsome scissors, axes and daggers. Tom held up his own shining swords as the crowd clapped.

In the audience there were men in white togas, children in tunics and women with the most elaborately curled hair Tom had ever seen. Tom felt like they were all cheering for him.

Now I know how football players feel when they're walking on to the pitch, Tom thought. It was so exciting, he almost forgot he was there to fight a battle to the death.

"This is beyond brilliant!" he told Isis.

Isis pretended to aim her bow at the crowd. "It will only be beyond brilliant *if* I get my amulet and don't get killed... again!"

Behind them came the actors whose job it was to put on plays in between fights, to keep the crowd entertained. Finally, at the very back of the parade, came Josephus and the animals.

"I thought the animals weren't fighting," Tom said to Isis.

"They're not," Isis said. "But Josephus told me that Atillius wanted the animals as part of the parade to impress the spectators."

Tom glanced back at the cages that had been wheeled into the arena. There, spread out on the best bit of straw and looking very much like the cat of a princess, was Cleo.

He nudged Isis. "Look who's decided to join in!"

Isis grinned and waved at her pet. "My fluffpot! Look! Now *there's* an impressive beast!"

Tom peered at the normally ferocious lions, alligator, tigers and two bears, in the cages by Josephus. He noticed that all the animals were huddled in the corner of their cages. No roaring. No growling. And certainly no snarling.

"You know," Tom said, "they still seem scared of Cleo."

"Of course they do. Quite right too," Isis said, twanging the string on her bow.

★

Once the parade had been all the way around the amphitheatre, the trumpeters lined up. Silence fell like a blanket on the crowd as the musicians tooted an important-sounding fanfare. Tom's skin erupted into little goosebumps and then...

"Put your hands together for the star of the show!" Atillius cried. "The great, the astounding, the winner of his last thirteen fights, the one and only... HILARUS!"

The crowd sprang to their feet, cheering and clapping so loudly that Tom had to cover his ears with his hands.

In strode Hilarus. He was punching the air and chuckling to himself, as if fighting off five gladiators at once was the best joke he'd ever heard.

"'Cheerful is the one you need to find,'" Tom said, remembering the riddle. "I can see where Hilarus gets his name from."

"He won't be so cheerful when we get the amulet from his shield," Isis said.

Hilarus shone in the sunshine as though he was on fire. Chunks of honey-coloured amber, like precious candy, had been studded into his pure-gold breastplate and sewn into his skirt. Even the cloth of his tunic beneath the armour looked like it had been spun from gold thread.

"Oooh," cooed the crowd. Everybody
jostled and elbowed one another out of the
way to get a better look at the gleaming,
golden gladiator.

102

Tom was straining to see too, but not because Hilarus was his hero. There it was: a glittering orange lump in the middle of the gladiator's round shield. More jewel-like than the amber that surrounded it, the stone was unmistakeably ancient and magical.

"Do you see what I see?" Tom asked, breath coming short with excitement.

Isis nodded, her eyes wide. She gripped Tom's arm. "It's the first amulet."

CHAPTER 8

HILARUS

"Hurry up, already. When is it going to be our turn?" huffed Isis, pacing up and down. "Princesses don't like to be kept waiting."

After the parade, the *catervarii* had been brought to a chamber under the arena.

Tom kicked the sawdust strewn around the stone floor as they waited to be called into the ring. He wasn't in such a rush for a showdown with the legendary gladiator. He could just glimpse Rufus's sandal-clad feet, planted at the top of the same stone stairs that would lead him and Isis back into the fray.

Tom's heart was beating so loudly he wondered if the grumpy-looking guards flanking them could hear it. Listening to the crowd's gasps and the clashing of weapons, he realised how dangerous their plan was.

Suddenly, the crowd above them burst into deafening applause. Judging from the shouts of 'Hilarus! Hilarus!' the famous gladiator had won another fight.

"End of the bout," one guard said to the other. "And a messy one. The slaves will have a job getting all that blood out of the sand."

Tom gave a little whimper.

"Scaredy cat," Isis said. "I'm not the least bit frightened." But she was still pacing and

105

fidgeting with the scales on her armour. Tom was fairly certain that she *was* nervous. Just like him. But she was doing her best not to show it.

"Listen up, you lot!" Isis announced to Tom and the three other fighters who would face Hilarus. "We're going to win. I don't give two hoots about this Hilary! That big oaf is no match for me!"

Just then, footsteps clicked from the direction of the stairs. Rufus returned. Tom gulped and breathed heavily through his nose.

"All right, slaves," Rufus said to the *catervarii*. "You're on next."

In their group were Tom, Isis, a net-fighting *retiarius* who looked as though he ate children for breakfast, a *scissor* who was at least six feet tall and had arms like giant hams. The last member of the group was an *eques*, a fighter on horseback, like Isis. Only this man's head was so big, Tom was amazed Rufus had found a helmet to fit him. He carried a long lance and would start the fight.

"Fight bravely," Rufus said. "Remember that you're there to give the crowd a good time." He grinned at Tom and Isis and added, "So try not to die too soon."

★

As they marched up the stairs and back outside into the sunshine, Tom heard a foghorn of a voice booming across the amphitheatre.

"And now, brace yourselves for the highlight of the show brought to you by Atillius's Expandable Loincloths. It is time for five *catervarii* to face the undefeated,

107

the blessed-by-the-gods, the golden man-mountain that iiiiisssss... HILARUS!"

It was quite an introduction, Tom thought. He watched as the hero of the show strutted around the arena in his golden armour and feathered helmet, waving to the adoring crowds.

"He looks like a giant chicken," Isis scoffed.

"Well, if he's a chicken, that makes us sitting ducks," Tom said.

Hilarus played up to the spectators' ear-splitting cheering by cartwheeling, clowning around and generally being a show-off.

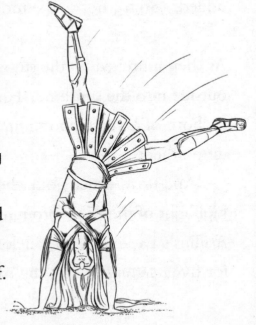

Meanwhile, his servants were collecting the money and gifts that the crowd were throwing into the arena for their hero.

The trumpeter led the musicians in a fast-paced tune and suddenly it was time for the fight to begin. Hilarus stood before the *catervarii* with a grim face. He raised his broad sword up high. In his other hand he held his round shield, complete with the sparkling amulet centrepiece.

"Attack!" Rufus cried behind them.

The enormous-headed *eques* was the first to spring forward on his horse. Hilarus turned to face his opponent, holding his shield in front of his face as the *eques's* long lance flew through the air towards him. The lance missed, clattering to the ground. Worse still for the horseman, a harsh trumpeting noise rang out unexpectedly somewhere in the arena. His horse reared up, whinnying and clearly terrified. The spooked horse streaked out of the amphitheatre, with his rider clinging on for dear life, leaving nothing but a cloud of dust in its wake.

"Disqualified!" Atillius barked.

Isis looked at Tom with narrowed eyes. "Four against one now..."

Next came the *scissor*, creeping forward with his double-bladed weapon. He lunged at Hilarus, wielding the heavy blades through the air as though they were as light as feathers.

"He's good," Tom said, nodding his approval.

But Hilarus twisted and turned, this way and that, tumbling backwards like a gymnast out of harm's reach. Suddenly the strong, meaty arms of the scissor fighter were of no use, as Hilarus wedged his own sword between the two blades of his opponent's weapon. With a sharp flick of his wrist, Hilarus prised the double-bladed sword out of his opponent's hands and tossed it through the air like a toy.

The defeated gladiator stumbled backwards and groaned aloud, as his only means of defence hit the ground with a *clank*!

The crowd erupted into deafening applause, and cheered for their hero.

"Three against one," Isis said, looking over at the net fighter who was baring a mouthful of rotten teeth. "Good job this isn't a beauty contest. He'd never win."

Tom eyed Hilarus warily. He was smiling broadly and waving to his adoring fans. Unruffled, unhurt, hardly breaking a sweat. And there was the amulet, safe in the middle of his shield, dazzling orange in the afternoon sunshine.

Tom gripped his swords in his sweaty hands. He muttered under his breath, "Have I got what it takes to be a hero?"

As if in answer, Anubis's mocking laughter rang shrilly in his ears.

"A mere boy like you? A hero? Ha ha

ha!" Sneering, snorting guffaws blocked out the noise of the cheering crowd. "Are you serious? What can *you* do?"

"I can try my best!" Tom shouted.

Anubis's voice fell silent. The god was nowhere to be seen.

Come on, Tom. Remember to breathe, he told himself. *Keep your cool. Hilarus is just a normal guy. Imagine him looking stupid in his undies, like Mr Brain-ache Braintree when he tells you off for daydreaming in Maths.*

Sadly for Tom, Hilarus was anything but a normal guy. Close up, he was a giant. Worse than that. He looked like a giant who ate an entire cow at every meal. As he gripped his broad sword, the muscles in his forearms stood out like fat lengths of rope. His neck was as thick as a tree trunk!

To his left, Isis's horse stamped and

whinnied. To his right, the net fighter was gnashing his teeth.

"Attack!" Rufus shouted some way behind him.

Hilarus gave a battle cry that was so scary, Tom was sure he could feel his heart racing around his chest looking for a place to hide. The golden giant thundered towards

him. But fear made Tom suddenly braver. He remembered his plan.

It's now or never! Tom thought. "Look out, Hilarus!" he shouted. "It's helicopter time!"

Tom lifted both swords into the air as he spun round. Tom whirled across the arena towards Hilarus like a kitchen blender gone mad. He hoped that Hilarus was getting dizzy so that Isis could grab the amulet.

But then the net fighter swung his net around in the air like a lasso and released it. The net swooshed past Tom's head and then down over Hilarus... and his shield!

"Ah, get it off me!" Hilarus bellowed. He strained and struggled under the heavy net, trying to throw it off.

"Ha ha ha! Not so cheerful now, are you, Hilarus?" Isis called out. "But you do look pretty funny!"

"I'll keep him busy – you get the amulet," Tom hissed at Isis.

He lunged forward and slapped the flat of his right sword hard against Hilarus's breastplate.

"Ha! Take that!" Tom shouted.

Hilarus jeered at him from under his net. "Trying to tickle me, are you, boy? You don't look as if you've got the courage to defeat the great Hilarus!"

He suddenly threw himself towards Tom. A writhing mass of giant shoulders and kicking legs sent Tom tumbling. With ice-cold dread, Tom felt Hilarus's strong grip close around his ankle.

"Who's laughing now?" Hilarus snarled.

CHAPTER 9
A SPEEDY EXIT

"Get off him, you big clown!" Isis shouted at Hilarus.

Tom looked up. Isis had an arrow stretched tight against the string of her bow. She was ready to strike. The arrow whizzed through the air. *Doink!* It glanced off Hilarus's helmet. Hilarus released Tom's ankle from his vice-like grip. Tom scuttled away quickly and watched as the hero stumbled to his feet, clutching at his head. He seemed dazed.

The crowd's frantic cheering for Hilarus hushed to a low murmur. Then came the booing and hissing.

"Oi! He's a legend. Leave him alone!" Tom heard a man shout.

"I hope you fall off your horse," another bellowed at Isis.

"Hilarus!" came a girl's voice. "We love you. Come on! Grind them into flour!"

We've almost got the amulet, Tom thought. *Hilarus isn't so invincible after all.*

But in order to get at the shield, they needed to cut a hole in the net. Tom ran in and slashed at Hilarus with both swords. The swords were sharp, cutting through easily.

The gladiator suddenly stopped thrashing about like a fly caught in a spider's web.

119

Tom thought for a moment that he'd hurt him. But then the gladiator stood up tall, pushing the net off. *Uh oh*. Tom hadn't just cut a hole, he'd accidentally *freed* Hilarus!

All at once, heavy footsteps thundered behind Tom. He looked round to see the net fighter moving in for the kill at speed. Tom dodged out of the way as the two giants crashed into one another in a clash of metal and muscle.

"Kick him up the bum!" somebody in the crowd shouted.

Sure enough, Hilarus wrestled the net fighter to the ground and, as if to please his crowd of cheering fans, he kicked his opponent's bottom with his enormous gnarly foot.

Oof! The *retiarius* landed face first in the sand, sending one of his rotten teeth flying.

"You're not even worth blunting my sword for!" Hilarus bellowed.

"The *retiarius* is defeated!" Atillius announced.

The crowd collectively sighed with relief, then clapped and started cheering again. Now it was just Tom and Isis left.

Seeing Hilarus spring nimbly back into position, Tom started to twirl around again, readying himself for another attack. But the golden hero was quick off the mark. Hilarus

hurled himself headlong into Tom and
jabbed his broad sword up against Tom's two
spinning swords.

Clank! Hilarus knocked both swords right
out of Tom's hands. They clattered on the
ground several feet away.

"Oh no!" Tom cried. He turned to Isis.
"My swords! I'm unarmed." He watched,
as Hilarus approached with a wicked look
in his eyes. Any trace of good humour had
disappeared.

Tom stared desperately into the crowd.
The blood was rushing in his ears. *Come on,
Tom! Think!* he told himself.

Hilarus held out his sword, pointing to
Tom's heart. "Do you surrender?"

Tom looked at the sword's tip and then
at his chest. He opened his mouth, still
wondering what to say, when the words,

"*No way!*" popped out.

"That's the spirit, Tom!" Isis shouted. "Never surrender!"

She galloped up beside him and with a surprisingly strong arm, snatched him up into the saddle.

Once Tom was out of Hilarus's reach, Isis reined in her horse and dropped him gently to the ground. "Teamwork! Remember?"

she said, winking. "We're going to get that amulet!"

Isis drew her bow and aimed her arrow at Hilarus's grimacing face. He stood with his legs apart, bashing the hilt of his sword against his shield. Now he wasn't laughing – he was growling! The crowd was going wild, shouting for their hero to charge at the child on the horse.

"Think you can scare me?" Isis shouted to Hilarus. "I've seen worse than you!"

With her bow and arrow still trained on the golden gladiator, Isis galloped towards Hilarus.

"Go on, Isis! You can do it!" cheered Tom.

Hilarus barely had time to swing his sword at Isis. She yanked on her horse's reins, pulling it hard to Hilarus's left – the side of his shield arm. Just beyond his sword's reach, Isis leaned out of the saddle of her cantering horse. She gripped her arrow like a dagger and thrust it towards the amulet. Edging the sharp tip underneath the gem, Isis pushed with all her might and... FLIP!

"Got it!" she cried.

Tom watched as the amulet leaped free of its setting and hurtled through the air. The whole crowd gasped as the glittering, precious jewel flew across the arena.

It landed in the sand, right in front of the barrier that bordered the seating.

"It's mine!" Isis shouted. "We did it, Tom!"

But as Isis galloped over to the jewel, a girl sitting in the front row bent over the barrier and snatched up the amulet.

"No!" Tom shouted.

"Come back here so I can crush you!" Hilarus roared, sprinting after Isis.

Tom's heart was pounding again. He was unarmed. But Isis, who was arguing with the girl, had her back turned. And an angry Hilarus was closing the gap with his sword drawn.

I've got to distract him, Tom thought. He stuck his fingers in his mouth and let out a piercing wolf whistle. "Oi! Hilarious Hilary!" Tom cried. "Your leather skirt is tucked into your loincloth."

Hilarus stopped dead in his tracks and swung round to face Tom. "What did you say?" he said.

"Everyone can see your bum," Tom shouted. "Ha ha ha!"

The gladiator's face had turned an alarming shade of beetroot. Despite being called Hilarus, it didn't seem like the gladiator could take a joke. Tom was almost paralysed with fear, but he knew he had to keep taunting Hilarus. For Isis's sake!

"They all think you're an idiot now!" Tom yelled. "Big bum!"

Half of the crowd started to shout, "Don't listen to him, Hilarus!" The other half burst out laughing.

Hilarus tugged self-consciously at his leather skirt. "Are you making a mockery of me, boy?" He narrowed his eyes and started to stomp towards Tom. "I should have killed you when I had the chance."

Suddenly, the girl who had taken the amulet cried out, "Hilarus! Help me!"

Hilarus, only feet away from Tom, swung round.

The girl was waving the amulet in the air.

Isis had dismounted and leaped over the barrier. Her arrow was trained straight on the girl's heart.

The whole crowd gasped and fell silent.

"Get the amulet, Isis! You can do it!" Tom shouted.

"That's mine. Give it back!" Isis demanded, pulling the arrow back, ready to shoot.

The girl clutched the jewel close to her chest. "I will not," she said in a shaky voice. "This belongs to Hilarus and I'm his biggest fan."

Hilarus was charging like an angry bull back towards Isis now. The crowd were hurling insults at her and booing loudly.

Above the mayhem, Atillius's voice boomed, "Guards! Stop the games! Seize those children!"

Tom felt the colour drain from his face as a swarm of spear-wielding stewards streamed down the tiers of seating towards him. There was no time to lose.

Spying his two swords lying abandoned in the dust, Tom ran over and grabbed the hilts. *Great. At least I'm armed again*, he thought. Then, sprinting towards Isis so fast that he was sure his lungs would explode, Tom called out, "Get the amulet! It's time to go!"

The stewards were closing in, spears at the ready. Tom could feel their shadows bearing down on him.

"What are you waiting for?" Atillius barked. "Clap those children in chains! I'll feed them to the lions myself."

The stewards lowered their spears so they were pointing right at Tom and Isis's bellies.

A voice boomed out, "No, Atillius! These two are mine!"

Hilarus pushed the stewards aside and treated the girl who was his biggest fan to a dazzling grin. With a short, sharp blow from his sword, he knocked the bow and arrow clean out of Isis's hands.

"Now, Isis!" Tom hissed through gritted teeth.

Isis reached out and swiped the amulet from the girl's hand. The girl was so distracted by her idol standing close to her that she didn't even seem to notice her trophy had gone.

Isis flashed the orange amulet at Tom and gave him a nod. Together, they started to race towards the exit.

"It was nice knowing you all," Isis called to Hilarus and the stewards, "but we're very busy people and it's time to go."

Tom was just about to join hands with Isis when he froze in horror.

"Er, Isis," he said. "Aren't you forgetting something?"

Isis looked blank for a moment, and then despair spread across her face. "Cleo!" she wailed. "We can't leave without my fluffpot!"

CHAPTER 10
TOP CAT

Tom knew they had missed their chance. It was no use. The guards had caught up with them and they were surrounded on all sides by tall stewards with mean-looking faces and glinting spears. How would they get to Cleo now?

Tom noticed that the stewards' togas were dazzling white and draped in careful folds, and the men wore beaded sandals on their feet.

"Great sandals, guys," Tom said, trying to say anything that might distract the stewards long enough for him take a swipe at them.

A couple of the stewards actually looked down at their feet and smiled, but it wasn't enough to make them drop their spears.

"Nice try, prison scum!" one of the stewards said, shaking his spear. "Throw down your weapons or I'll skewer you like a kebab."

"We need to get past them," Isis cried. "I've got to get to Cleo!"

The men were closing in on them.

Tom looked about him. Guards were everywhere. He held out his two swords even though his tired arms were shaking with the weight.

"Just try to push them back towards the prisoners' quarters," Tom said to Isis.

"How? They took my bow and arrows, remember?" she said.

Tom racked his brains for a solution.

"Kick sand at them," he shouted.

Isis grinned and nodded. Together they started to kick sand at the stewards. Clouds of dust billowed round, making them cough.

"I can't see!" a steward gasped.

Tom slashed at the stewards with his left sword. There was a clash of metal as he tried to force their spears aside.

"Take that!" he yelled. He swung his sword low, chopping the long wooden shafts of five spears clean in half.

Isis aimed a few brutal kicks at the shins of several of the stewards and they buckled over, groaning and clutching their legs.

"Sounds like that hurt!" Isis cried, grinning mischievously.

Then she grabbed handfuls of dust and flung them in the men's faces. She snatched up one of the spear heads from the ground and slashed at the brooches that held the men's togas together. The stewards were soon tangled up in their own clothing, cowering with embarrassment before the guffawing spectators.

Tom saw their chance. "Run!" he shouted to Isis.

They made good progress back towards the entrance to the prisoners' quarters, but more stewards appeared from the rows of seats and chased after them.

Tom and Isis sprinted down the stone stairs and pelted down the corridors that led to the animals' enclosure, hurdling anything that stood in their way.

"Did we lose them?" Isis gasped.

Tom looked behind him. "No! Faster!"

The men were gaining on them.

Ahead, Tom spotted Josephus fetching a bucket of water.

"Help us!" he shouted.

Josephus looked round, startled. He nodded as Tom and Isis skidded to a halt by the heavy wooden door.

"This thing weighs a tonne. Push together," Josephus said.

They all wedged their shoulders up against the door and put their full weight behind it until it began to inch inwards.

"Quick! They're coming!" Tom wailed.

"There they are!" the stewards bellowed.

Five men bowled along the corridor towards Tom and Isis. There was a *whizz!* as a spear shot through the air towards them.

"Duck!" Josephus barked.

Bedoinnng! went the spear as it impaled itself into the wood of the door. It was a near miss but they had the door open now.

"Take us straight to Cleo!" Isis commanded Josephus.

They sped past the alligator and a cage full of tigers to Cleo's special spot. She was sound asleep, curled up on a cozy bed of hay

137

at the back of the lion's cage. The lions were huddled in a far corner, whimpering.

"Fluffpot!" Isis cried. Cleo woke up and stretched lazily. The men were almost upon them now. Josephus threw a bale of hay in their path to slow them down.

"It's no use," Tom said in frustration. "They're going to capture us! There's nowhere left to run!" His heart was beating so wildly, he could hardly hear himself think. Next to him, Isis was trembling like jelly. Tom searched his mind for a last-ditch escape route.

"Hang on!" he said to Isis. "Aren't the wild animals terrified of Cleo?"

Isis nodded frantically. "Yes! Yes!" she said. "Somehow they know she's a ghost!"

"I've got it," Tom said. He turned to Josephus. "Release the animals!"

Josephus was wide-eyed. His forehead glistened with sweat. "Are you mad?" he cried. "They'll eat you alive."

A spear landed with a rattle at their feet.

"We've got no other choice, Josephus," Tom said. "As long as we've got Cleo on our side, we should be safe. It's the only way we can escape the stewards!"

Josephus still didn't look convinced. The alligator started snapping its enormous jaws. It thrashed its tail from side to side. The tigers paced in their cage, growling. The lions started to roar and fling themselves against the bars of their enclosures.

The men were almost upon them with spears and swords.

"Give me the key!" Isis shouted, wrestling it out of Josephus's hands.

Isis held up the key and taunted the

139

guards. "Time for walkies!" she cried,
unlocking the cages.

The animals bolted out of their cages.
Cleo trotted out after them, her tail held
proudly in the air. But instead of attacking,
the alligator and the lions backed away
nervously from Cleo. The little cat hissed
at them, then the animals fled down the
corridor leading to the arena – trying to
get as far away from Cleo as they could.
Terrified, the stewards screamed and ran
the other way.

Josephus shook his head in amazement. "I've seen some strange things in my time, but this is the strangest yet."

"Will you be OK?" Tom asked him.

"Hilarus will deal with the animals," Josephus said. He held up a bucket of meat. "And if you give them some of this, they're tame as kittens."

Cleo jumped into Isis's arms and nuzzled her mistress. She pawed at Isis's tightly closed fist. Isis unfurled her fingers to reveal the orange amulet she still held in the palm of her hot, sweaty hand.

"What should we do now?" she asked, fixing Tom with wide, puzzled eyes.

Tom reached out and touched the amulet. It began to glow bright orange.

Wind started to whip around the animals' quarters. The gust furled around his ankles, quickly turning into a tornado that twisted around Tom, Isis and Cleo. There was a sucking sensation and Tom just had time to say, "Thank you and goodbye," to a bewildered-looking Josephus before he felt himself being whisked into a tunnel. Then the wind blew so hard that Tom was forced to squeeze his eyes shut as he flew through space and time...

CHAPTER 11
HOME SWEET HOME

When Tom opened his eyes again, all traces of the animals' quarters and the Roman Coliseum were gone. He was back in his bedroom. He looked over at Isis and Cleo. They'd made it back safely as well, but they were in their mummy's bandages again.

Isis examined her wrappings. "It's nice not to be in chains any more," she said, sighing. "But I'm not happy to see *these* grotty things again."

Cleo jumped stiffly on to her lap and pawed at a piece of Isis's loose fabric.

"It's such a shame we only get to have our proper bodies back when we're on a quest!" Isis moaned.

Tom looked around the silent room. He ran his finger over the books on his bookshelf, his fossil collection and his knight figurines. He touched the monitor of his computer, which was still open on his search on Ancient Egypt.

"Feels weird to be back, doesn't it?" he said, glancing at his clock. "Anubis was right about the time though. Look!" he pointed to the glowing digital display. "Same time as when we left."

Isis held up the amulet to the light and watched the magical jewel sparkle, scattering orange patterns on to the bedroom wall.

"It's so pretty," she cooed, "And it would look so lovely in a necklace—"

"Don't even think about it!" said Tom.

Suddenly the floor shook, the light flickered, thunder rumbled and a strong wind sent Tom's curtains flapping.

"Oh, brilliant! Here we go again!" Tom muttered.

The door of Tom's wardrobe burst open. The huge figure of Anubis pushed Tom's school uniform aside and loomed from the gloom, his red eyes flashing and his arms crossed.

"Still haven't learned your lesson, Princess Isis?" the god growled.

Anubis flicked his tongue over his muzzle and eyed the glittering amulet greedily.

Tom watched as the god of the Underworld advanced out of the shadows.

He was so tall that he could barely fit in Tom's room. Tom felt certain he was on a collision course with his lampshade.

"Mind out," Tom said, pointing.

Anubis took two steps forward and – *kwang!* – he hit his head. "OW!" he said, rubbing his pointy ears. The jackal-headed god slapped the light angrily. "What is this sorcery?" he asked crossly.

Isis giggled. "It's not sorcery, its electricity," she said smugly.

"You think you're clever, do you?" Anubis roared, blasting them with his meaty doggy breath.

"Yes, actually, we do," Isis said.

"Well, a clever little girl would hand over that amulet right now – before I blast her straight back to Ancient Rome!" the furious god bellowed.

"Go on, Isis," urged Tom.

"All right, all right," said Isis, sulkily dropping the glowing amulet into the god's hand. "But I still think it would look much better on me."

"ENOUGH!" raged Anubis. He circled the two children menacingly, as if deciding whether or not to tear their heads off. It made Tom feel almost homesick for the lions and alligator in the Roman animal enclosure. At least they were scared of Cleo, but now the terrified cat was hiding under Tom's bed, her bandaged paws covering her eyes.

Anubis leaned in towards Tom and Isis and growled, "You have found and recovered the first amulet. But your next challenge will be much, much harder. Your adventures in Ancient Rome will seem like

a mere game." He threw back
his head and laughed
wildly, showing
his sharp
teeth.

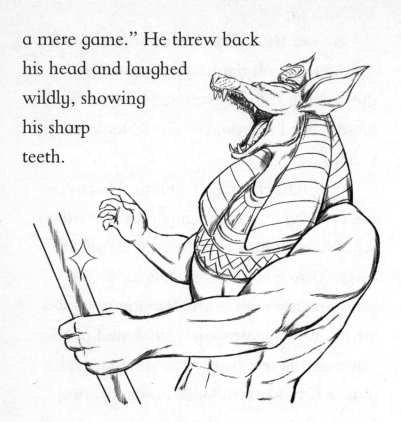

Then the ground shook and the god of
the Underworld disappeared with a small
explosion that left a corner of Tom's new
carpet with a burned patch.

"My mum is really not going to be pleased

about that," said Tom gloomily, sniffing the acrid air and kicking at the mark.

Isis stiffly leaned back on Tom's bed. Her joints made a horrible cracking noise. A piece of her little finger fell off, landing on the carpet.

"Or that," said Tom, handing Isis her finger and brushing away the pile of dust it left behind.

Isis jammed the finger back on her hand hastily. "I'm soooo tired," she said, lying down flat on her back with her hands crossed over her chest. Cleo curled up beside her. Within moments, both cat and princess were snoring so loudly that Tom wondered for a moment if Anubis had conjured up a small earthquake in the room.

"I guess that's what you call sleeping like the dead," Tom said. "That's fine. Don't worry about me. I'll just try to get some rest on my burned carpet, shall I?"

Tom shuffled on the floor. He was struggling to get comfortable.

Come on, Tom, he told himself. *You slept on a stone floor for days, with another slave's toes practically stuffed up your nostrils! This is like a palace by comparison.*

In the quiet and comforting dark of his room, Tom thought about his Roman adventure. He had trained to fight as a gladiator! How exciting was that?

He remembered the heavy feel of the swords in his hands and the roar of the crowd. *For a moment there, I almost had Hilarus.*

Tom smiled at the moon that shone through a chink in his curtains. As sleep started to take him, he thought of the gladiator's boring breakfast of dried fruit and porridge. Wrinkling his nose, he imagined eggs, bacon and baked beans instead.

Five more amulets to find, he pondered. *I wonder where our next adventure will be?* Maybe they would go to Ancient Greece or Ancient Egypt, or even back to medieval times...

He opened one eye and peered through the gloom at the sleeping forms of Isis and Cleo. Tom knew one thing for sure – with the undead mummies of an Egyptian princess and her cat around, life certainly wasn't going to be boring!

TURN THE PAGE TO . . .

➤ **Meet the REAL gladiators!**

➤ **Find out fantastic FACTS!**

WHO WERE THE MIGHTIEST GLADIATORS?

Hilarus was actually a *real* gladiator! Find out more about him and other fearsome fighters.

HILARUS was a slave who belonged to a troupe of gladiators owned by the Emperor Nero. He won 13 wreathes for his victories, making him one of Ancient Rome's most successful fighters. He was eventually defeated by a novice gladiator named Marcus Attilius. However, Hilarus fought so bravely in their fight that he was spared death and given his freedom.

SPARTACUS was probably the most famous gladiator who ever lived. He became a slave as punishment for running away from the Roman army and was forced to fight as a gladiator.

In 73 BC, Spartacus ran away again. For two years, he and an army of slaves fought off the much-bigger Roman army. Eventually, Spartacus was captured and killed but he is remembered as a skilled military leader.

FLAMMA, meaning 'The Flame', was a slave from Syria who fought as a secatur. During his life, he won 21 battles and drew 9 times.

The most amazing thing about Flamma is that he was offered his freedom four times, but each time he chose to remain a gladiator and keep fighting because he liked the attention so much! He died aged 30 in his 34th fight. Maybe he should have retired!

EMPEROR COMMODUS ruled Rome between AD 180 – 192 but also enjoyed fighting as a gladiator. He especially liked fighting wild animals and is said to have killed 100 lions in one day!

Emperor Commodus was quite a show-off. Underneath a giant statue of himself he wrote that he had defeated 12,000 men! Some of his success was probably because he was the emperor and his opponents were scared to defeat him.

FANTASTIC FACTS

Impress your friends with these facts about
Ancient Rome.

➤ Only children from wealthy families
would be educated. Many were
tutored at home and schools were only
for boys. Punishments were severe
and some schools even used slaves to
hold the children down to be whipped.
Ouch!

➤ Dinner time was known as Cena and
it could last for hours. Ancient Romans
would eat dormice, sea urchins and
even peacock tongues.
Er, sounds tasty…

➤ Doctors would sometimes go to extreme lengths to find out what was wrong with a patient, by tasting their poo or drinking their wee.
How gross is that?!

➤ Cobwebs were used to stop cuts bleeding.
Bet you're glad we have plasters now?

➤ During the 3rd Century over 20 Roman emperors ruled were assassinated.
What a deadly job!

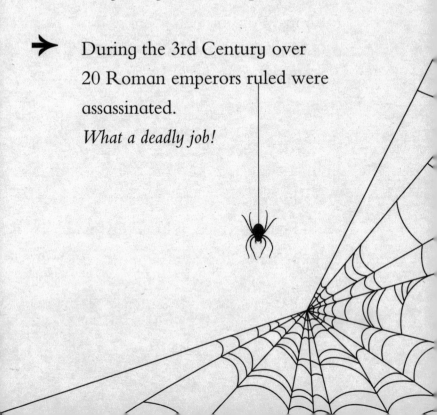